A PERFECT DAY

GREENWILLOW BOOKS
AN IMPRINT OF HARPERCOLLINS*PUBLISHERS*

FOR JUNE, WITH SPECIAL LOVE

I would like to thank my friends Eric Dekker
and Erika Bradfield for their help, and also
Minna Eloranta for her assistance in making
the pictures in this book.

A PERFECT DAY
COPYRIGHT © 2007 BY REMY CHARLIP
ALL RIGHTS RESERVED. MANUFACTURED IN CHINA.
WWW.HARPERCOLLINSCHILDRENS.COM

WATERCOLOR WASHES ON ARCHES PAPER WERE USED
TO PREPARE THE FULL-COLOR ART.
THE TEXT TYPE IS ALBERTUS.

LIBRARY OF CONGRESS CATALOGING-IN-PUBLICATION DATA
CHARLIP, REMY.
A PERFECT DAY / BY REMY CHARLIP.
    P.   CM.
"GREENWILLOW BOOKS."
SUMMARY: A PARENT AND CHILD SPEND A PERFECT DAY
TOGETHER, FROM SUNRISE TO NIGHTFALL.
ISBN-I0: 0-06-051972-X (TRADE BDG.) ISBN-I3: 978-0-06-051972-8 (TRADE BDG.)
ISBN-I0: 0-06-051973-8 (LIB. BDG.) ISBN-I3: 978-0-06-051973-5 (LIB. BDG.)
[I. PARENT AND CHILD—FICTION. 2. DAY—FICTION.
3. STORIES IN RHYME.] I. TITLE.
PZ8.3.C386PE 2006 [E]—DC22 2004052350

FIRST EDITION 10 9 8 7 6 5 4 3 2

 GREENWILLOW BOOKS

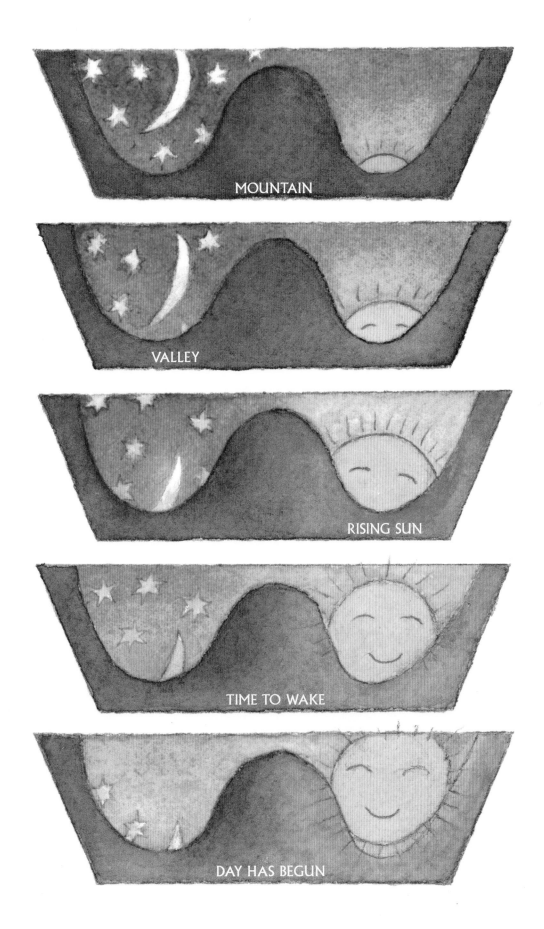

MOUNTAIN

VALLEY

RISING SUN

TIME TO WAKE

DAY HAS BEGUN

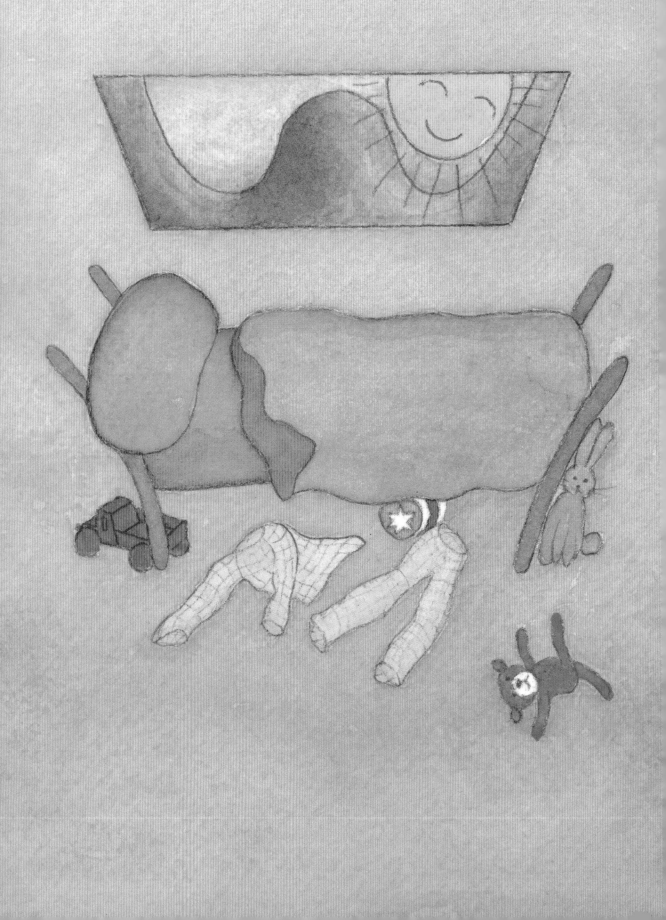

AT BREAKFAST

WE COULD TALK ABOUT...

HOW WE MIGHT GO

FOR A WALKABOUT.

WATCH THE CLOUDS...

IMAGINING...

WE CAN DO MOST ANYTHING.

TO EAT SOME LUNCH.

SING AND DANCE

WITH A FRIENDLY BUNCH.

CUDDLE UP UPON MY LAP.

CLOSE YOUR EYES

AND TAKE A NAP.

PAINT SOME PICTURES

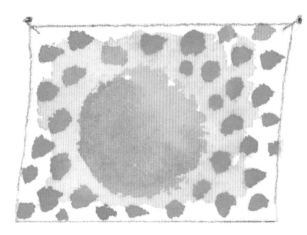 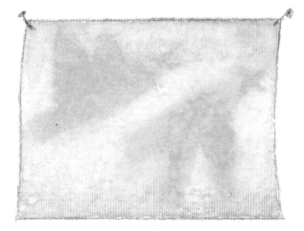

HANG THEM

OF IT ALL.

ON THE KITCHEN WALL.

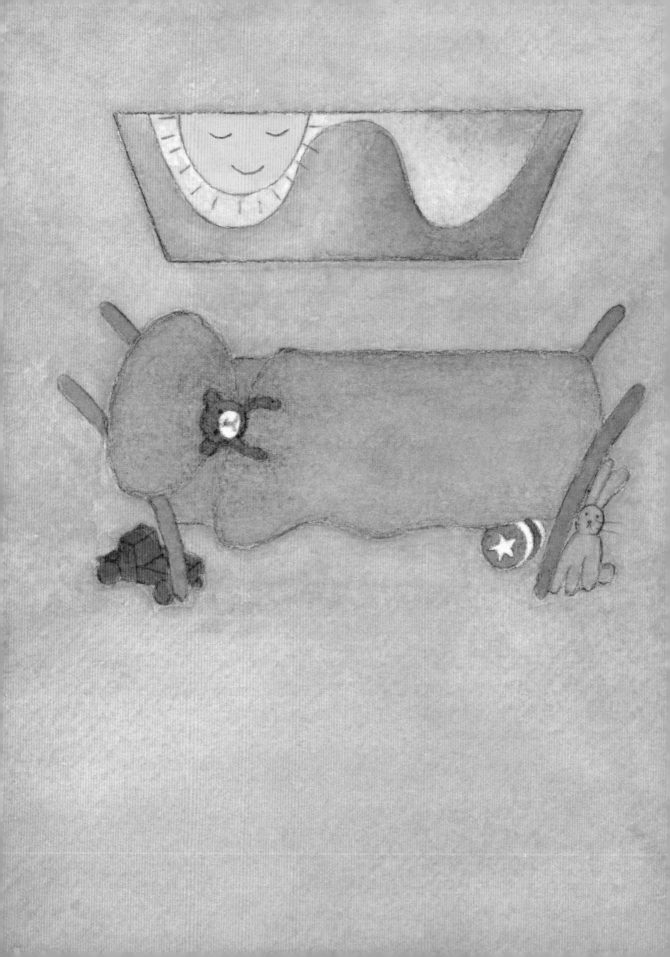

HAVE A BIT TO EAT AND DRINK.

READ FROM PICTURE BOOKS

AND THINK.

TOMORROW IS ANOTHER DAY.

TOMORROW WE CAN LAUGH

AND PLAY.

BUT NOW, STRETCH OUT

I'LL TUCK YOU IN,

INTO YOUR BED.

MY SLEEPYHEAD.

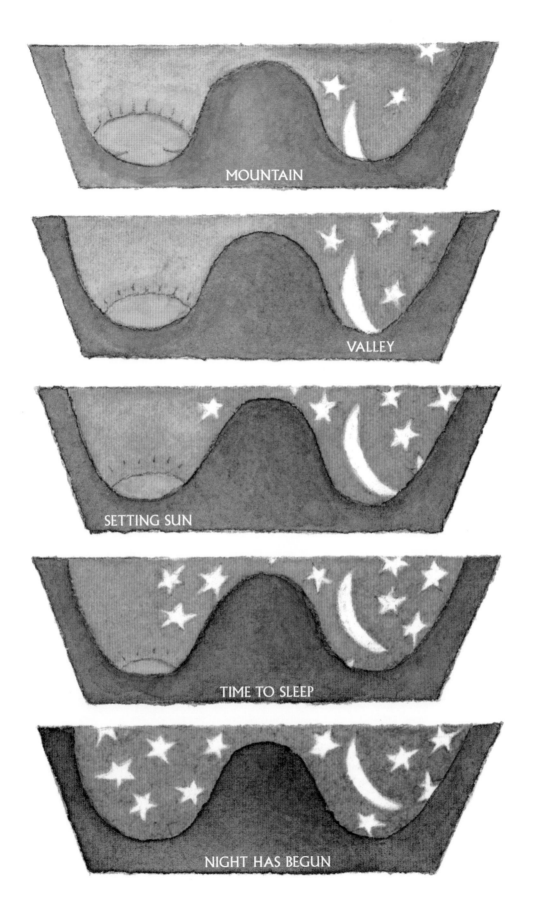

MOUNTAIN

VALLEY

SETTING SUN

TIME TO SLEEP

NIGHT HAS BEGUN

Remy Charlip

SAYS HE WAS FORTUNATE TO HAVE BEGUN HIS CAREER
ILLUSTRATING THE WORK OF TWO BRILLIANT PICTURE BOOK
PIONEERS: MARGARET WISE BROWN (THE DEAD BIRD)
AND RUTH KRAUSS (A MOON OR A BUTTON).
IN 1957 HIS OWN PICTURE BOOK WHERE IS EVERYBODY?
WAS CHOSEN BY THE NEW YORK PUBLIC LIBRARY
AS A "DISTINGUISHED READER," ALONG WITH THE CAT
IN THE HAT AND LITTLE BEAR. SINCE THEN HE HAS DONE
MORE THAN THIRTY BOOKS, INCLUDING SUCH MODERN
CLASSICS AS FORTUNATELY, I LOVE YOU, ARM IN ARM,
MOTHER MOTHER I FEEL SICK, AND, MORE RECENTLY,
SLEEPYTIME RHYME AND BABY HEARTS AND BABY FLOWERS.
HIS AWARDS INCLUDE A BOSTON GLOBE-HORN BOOK AWARD,
BEST PICTURE BOOK AT THE BOLOGNA BOOK FAIR, THREE
INCLUSIONS IN THE NEW YORK TIMES "TEN BEST ILLUSTRATED
BOOKS OF THE YEAR," AND A GUGGENHEIM FELLOWSHIP.

HE WAS HONORED BY THE LIBRARY OF CONGRESS
IN AN EVENING "CELEBRATION OF REMY CHARLIP,"
AND WITH A MAJOR EXHIBITION OF HIS PAINTINGS
AND DRAWINGS AT THE SAN FRANCISCO MAIN LIBRARY,
WHERE HE WAS ALSO NAMED A "LITERARY LAUREATE"
AND THEIR FIRST "ARTIST IN RESIDENCE."

REMY CHARLIP LIVES IN SAN FRANCISCO, CALIFORNIA.
WWW.REMYCHARLIP.COM